MRS. MORGAN'S LAWN

HOORAY FOR SHANE!

Barney Saltzberg
10-5-96

MRS. MORGAN'S LAWN

Barney Saltzberg

HYPERION BOOKS FOR CHILDREN
New York

For information address Hyperion Books for Children,
114 Fifth Avenue, New York, New York 10011.
FIRST EDITION
1 3 5 7 9 10 8 6 4 2

Library of Congress Cataloging-in-Publication Data
Saltzberg, Barney.
Mrs. Morgan's lawn / Barney Saltzberg—1st ed.
p.   cm.
Summary: Mrs. Morgan, who is very fussy and protective about her
front yard, confiscates all the soccer balls, baseballs, and other
kinds of balls that land there while neighborhood children are
playing.
ISBN 1-56282-423-6—ISBN 1-56282-424-4 (lib. bdg.)
[1. Neighborliness—Fiction.   2. Balls (Sporting goods)—Fiction.]
I. Title.
PZ7.S1152Mr   1993
[E]—dc20   92-54873   CIP   AC

The artwork for each picture is prepared using pen and ink, colored pencil, and acrylic paint.
This book is set in 16-point Cushing Book.

Many people are a part of this book.
I want to thank them for their love and support:
Marcia Wernick; Laurie Sale; Sheldon Fogelman;
Barbara Bottner; Arthur Levine; Andrea Cascardi;
Hans Beimler; Stacey I. Levine; Anita Strick;
Peggy, Joy & George Rathmann; April Halprin Wayland;
Gary Bardovi; Linda Dimitroff; Vida Sculley;
Zach Saltzberg (for hat and modeling!);
Arthur Saltzberg (who was born while I wrote this book—
welcome to the world!!); Lily Saltzberg (art critic);
and especially my wife, Susan, for…everything!

In memory of Barbara Karlin and James Marshall,
who have been and will continue to be
a great source of inspiration.

Every time a ball lands on Mrs. Morgan's lawn, she keeps it.

Somewhere inside her house must be a closet full of balls.
What could she do with all of them?

Mrs. Morgan doesn't want anything touching her lawn.
She waits for leaves to fall, so she can catch them before they land.

My parents say that's how some people are.

Mrs. Morgan would keep her lawn inside her house if she could.

She moved her mailbox out by the sidewalk. I'm sure she's afraid the mail carrier might step on her lawn.

I know my parents say that's just how some people are, but I think some people are weird.

Last fall, we were playing with my brand-new purple-and-white soccer ball. The score was five to three when the worst possible thing happened. Philippe kicked the ball right over Renée's head.

Guess where it landed?

If that's how some people are, then some people are mean.
I bet Mrs. Morgan was born mean.

I told my parents I lost my new purple-and-white soccer ball. I said I wished Mrs. Morgan would take her lawn and move somewhere else.

My father suggested I speak with Mrs. Morgan and ask her to give me back my soccer ball.

I figured there must be an easier way to get the ball back.

I thought I would call Mrs. Morgan and tell her I was from a radio station that was having a contest to see who had the most soccer balls, footballs, tennis balls, and baseballs. I would tell her to put them all in a box on her front porch so the station's official counters could stop by and count them.

Or what if I hid inside a giant ball and rolled onto Mrs. Morgan's lawn? She would take me inside, and I would find out where the rest of the balls were. Then I would wait until she went to sleep and take all the balls back.

I tried to think of a game I would like that didn't need a ball....
I decided to speak to Mrs. Morgan.

Mrs. Morgan had a bad cold.

I told her that I was sorry and that I had tried to be careful and that it had been an accident every time my ball landed on her lawn.

I told her that her lawn had taken all of my green glow-in-the-dark tennis balls…plus, the professional leather football I got for my birthday…plus, four brand-new baseballs. And, finally, my favorite purple-and-white soccer ball.

She acted like she didn't know what I was talking about.

All she said was to make sure I didn't step on her lawn on my way out.

My parents said they were proud of me for speaking up.
I couldn't understand why. I didn't get any of the balls back.
I said I wished Mrs. Morgan would disappear!

The next morning Mrs. Morgan wasn't outside. I guess she still had a bad cold. Something was different about her lawn.

When my ball rolled onto Mrs. Morgan's lawn, nothing happened.
It just sat there.

I could actually play without worrying about losing my ball.
It was great!

After a few days I knew that something wasn't right. Mrs. Morgan would never want her lawn looking so bad.

I spent my afternoons hunting for my ball when it rolled onto her lawn because the leaves had piled so high.

I decided to rake the leaves.

The next day, Mrs. Morgan was back outside. She must have felt better. My entire ball collection was on my front lawn except for my new purple-and-white soccer ball.

I thanked Mrs. Morgan for returning my collection and asked if she had forgotten my purple-and-white soccer ball.

Mrs. Morgan kept raking.
She acted as if she couldn't hear me.
My parents would say that's how some people are.

I say...

some people are full of surprises!